HOW SPIDER SAVED VALENTINE'S DAY

BY ROBERT KRAUS

SCHOLASTIC INC.

New York Toronto London Auckland Sydney

for Parker

ISBN 0-590-33743-2

12 11 10 9 8 7 6 5 4 3 2 1   1   6 7 8 9/8 0 1/9

Printed in U.S.A.

It was Valentine's Day and I was hurrying to school.

I stopped at the store and bought a bag of valentine candy and the last two valentines on the counter.

I got to school just as the last bell rang,
and put my valentines in the valentine box.

One for Ladybug and one for Fly.

At recess I shared my valentine candy with Fly
and Ladybug.
Ladybug chose a heart that said KISS ME, and I really
would have liked to.

Greedy Fly took two hearts. One said FAR OUT
and the other said COOL.
"I sure am," said Fly.

I wondered if I should share the candy with the two
caterpillars who sat in the back.
They were always so hungry.
And I had forgotten to get them valentines!

"They're asleep," said Ladybug.
"They're always asleep," said Fly.
Sure enough, the two hungry caterpillars were sleeping
soundly with their big fur coats pulled over their heads.
"They just eat and sleep," said Fly. "Lazy bugs!"

Then the recess bell rang and we all hurried
back to the classroom to get our valentines.

Miss Quito, our teacher, reached in the valentine box and passed out the valentines.

I got one from Ladybug, one from Fly,
and one from each of the hungry caterpillars who
sat in the back.

Fly got one valentine from me, one from Ladybug, and one from each of the hungry caterpillars who sat in the back.

Ladybug got one valentine from me, one from Fly,
and one from each of the hungry caterpillars
who sat in the back.

All the valentines were passed out and
NOBODY had gotten a valentine for
the two caterpillars who sat in the back.
It was pathetic. They had been sleeping
so much we forgot they were there.

But they *were* there!
And it was too late to get them a valentine now.
Or was it?

The two caterpillars were still sound asleep.
Then I got an idea!
I took my candy hearts and pasted them all over Fly.

Then I borrowed Ladybug's lipstick and lipsticked myself all over.

I sucked in my breath until I looked like a heart.

"What about me?" asked Ladybug.

"You're so pretty, you're a valentine just as you are,"
I said.
"Now everybody jump into the valentine box."

Miss Quito put the lid on the box.
"Hey, I can't breathe!" shouted Fly.

Then Miss Quito took the lid off the box and we all leaped out shouting, "Happy Valentine's Day, hungry caterpillars!"

They woke up.
But would you believe it?
They weren't caterpillars anymore.
They were bea — u — ti — ful butterflies!

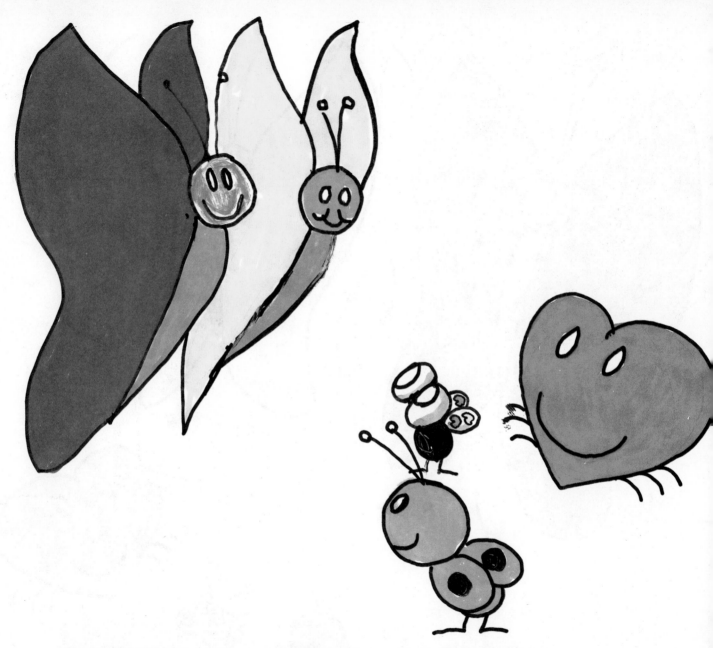

They thanked us for our valentines and we thanked
them for theirs.
Even Fly was nice.

Miss Quito played *I Love You Truly* on the piano
and we all sang.

"You've done it again, Spider," said Ladybug.
"Done what?" grumbled Fly. "Saved. . . ." said Miss Quito.
". . . Valentine's Day," said the two butterflies
who sat in the back.
And I guess I had.
I was very happy.

The End.